LADY AND
THE TRAMP

Ladybird Books

First edition

Published by Ladybird Books Ltd Loughborough Leicestershire UK

© 1992 The Walt Disney Company
Printed in England (3)

Jim Dear loved his wife, Darling, very much. One Christmas he gave her an adorable puppy called Lady.

Lady thought she was the luckiest dog alive to have such a lovely home.

Lady soon made
friends with the other
dogs in the neighbourhood.

But she didn't like Tramp, a scruffy mongrel. Lady thought he had very bad manners.

One day Lady's happy life came
to an end. Darling had a baby!

Darling gave all
her love and kisses
to the new arrival.
Lady was forgotten.

There was worse to come. Aunt Sara came to look after the baby while Jim and Darling were away.

She brought her Siamese cats
with her. Lady didn't like them
one bit.

The cats broke a vase, but Lady was blamed.

As a punishment, Lady was forced to wear a muzzle.

In a panic, Lady ran away.

She was chased by a pack of fierce dogs. With teeth bared, they drove Lady into a corner.

But Tramp leapt
to her rescue.

Then he got a friend to remove her
muzzle. Lady could smile again!

Lady realised at last that she had been wrong about Tramp. He was actually a gentleman in disguise!